Patiki, he the fish who floats flat on his side, he is patterned in the flowing painted rafter curves of kowhaiwhai painting.

Niho-taniwha is the triangle pattern woven into tukutuku reed panels. Taniwha is the terrible monster of the swamps, and these are the awful teeth of the Taniwha. (But some tribes call this pattern kaokao — the armpit!)

Purupuru-whetu is an ancient tukutuku shape. Its pattern is similar to roimata, the pattern of soft-falling raindrops.

Ngutu-kaka, the beak of the parrot, is a pattern often used in the white-wood clay-red soot-black flow of kowhaiwhai rafter design.

THE HOUSE OF THE PEOPLE

Told in the simple narrative style of the Maori orators of old, this is the story of the people of a kainga who decided that they needed a meeting house built on their spacious marae.

And the oldest tohunga agreed that they needed such a house and promised he would design and build it for them, and that it would be a house of wonder.

THE HOUSE OF THE PEOPLE won the Russell Clark award for the most distinguished illustrations in a children's book.

The same author and artist next collaborated on a book dealing with the making of a war canoe. Called *The Fish of Our Fathers,* this second book won for author and artist the prestigious N.Z. Children's Picture Story Book of the Year Award for 1985.

They have continued their co-operation and have completed a third book which describes the layout and building of a defensive pa on a hill. It is appropriately titled *The Home of the Winds.*

About the Author
Ron Bacon, Australian by birth but New Zealander by habit and long time residence, has written two adult novels, two books in co-operation with photographer Greg Riethmaier on their adopted city of Auckland, as well as several children's books, two in collaboration with artist Para Matchitt.

Married with three children, he is now Principal of a South Auckland primary school.

About the Artist
Robert Jahnke, a graduate of the Elam School of Fine Arts, Auckland, and the California Institute of the Arts, is an art teacher at Mangere College. He is married, with one child.

First published 1977 by William Collins
(New Zealand) Ltd.
This edition published 1983 by
Waiatarua Publishing
P.O. Box 87003 Meadowbank,
Auckland 5, New Zealand.

Reprinted 1986

First published in Great Britain 1986
by Child's Play (International) Ltd.

Typeset by Monoset Trade Services Limited,
Auckland.
Printed in Singapore.

ISBN 0-85953-300-X

The House of the People

Story by R. L. Bacon   Illustrations by R. H. G. Jahnke

Hear now, my mokopuna . . .

Published by Child's Play (International) Ltd

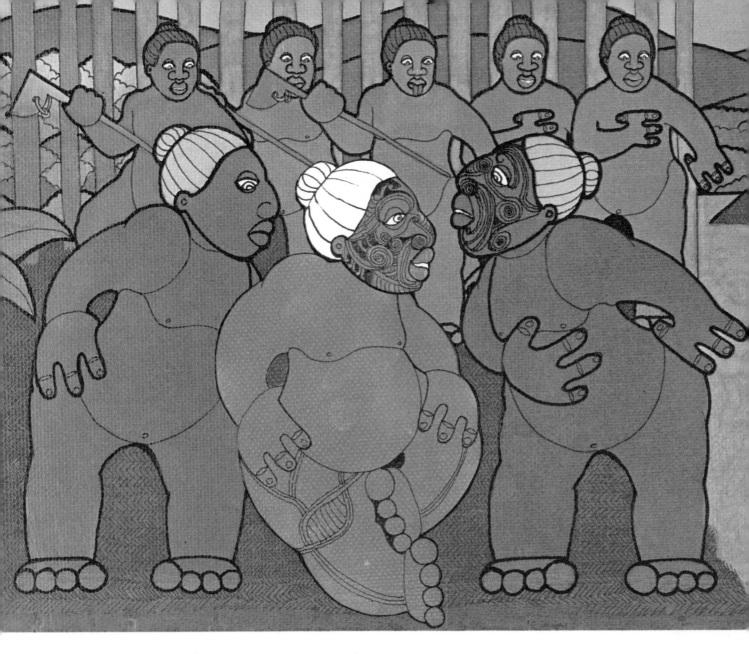

. . . hear how once in the long ago the people of the kainga met on their marae and they said, 'Aue! Here in our kainga we have a fine wide marae, a marae where our old people may meet and talk in the warm rays of Ra the sun, a marae where our fighting men may practise the haka and other arts of war, a marae where our maidens may dance the poi, where our women may tend the cooking fires. Ae,' said the people, 'we have such a marae, but for our marae we need a house.'

Then the people of the kainga spoke with the tohunga, saying, 'We need a house, a house where our people may meet when the dull dark nights of winter are come, a house where our children may hear tales of long ago, tales of taniwha and turehu, of goblins and gods and days long gone.'

And the oldest tohunga listened and he spoke to the people, 'Ae, such a house I shall build for you and it will be as no house has been before. A house of wonder it will be, and its name will be Te Whare o Nga Tangata Whenua, the House of the People.'

And the oldest tohunga said to himself, 'I shall go even to all the corners of our land to see those things I shall build into and pattern into this our house, to make this house a wonder for all to see. I shall go to the great sacred forest of Tane to think on the things I shall do to make the house truly a fine house for the people.'

And know, my mokopuna, that the time when the tohunga went out was in the time of Te Marama-mutu-whenua, the time of the last days of Marama the moon, when Marama lay quiet on her back in the pale morning sky, a thin slice of light in the clear morning sky, and the oldest tohunga said, 'Arara! Even as Marama lies in the sky, so shall I pattern the thin slice of the last days of Marama into the patterns of the house.'

Now know that the way to the great
forest of Tane lay along the smooth
sandy beach Taoneroa, and on the beach
the tohunga saw Patiki the flounder,
flying his flat fish way through the
shallow sandy pools, and the oldest
tohunga said, 'Ae, I see you, Patiki, flying
through the sea even as Manu, the kite of
the mokopuna, flies through air. You,
Patiki, you also shall I pattern into the
house to make the house truly a fine
house for the people.'

And on the beach Taoneroa were the fisher canoes pulled high up on the sand, and he saw the fisher-folk with their baskets of fish, Ika-moana the fish, children of Tangaroa, god of the sea. And the oldest tohunga said, 'Ae, Ika-moana the fish, children of Tangaroa, these too shall I make part of the house. The scales of Ika-moana shall I take and make for a pattern in the house.'

From the long sandy beach Taoneroa the oldest tohunga looked to the waters of the bay and he saw in the bay Pakeke the whale, Pakeke the great spouting fish of Tangaroa, Pakeke foaming the waters of the bay with his terrible tail, and the oldest tohunga said, 'Ae, I see you, great Pakeke. You too I see. You I shall not forget. You also shall I pattern into the house Te Whare o Nga Tangata Whenua, into the House of the People.'

On the edge of the cliff high above the bay, where Tawhirimatea, god of the winds, where Tawhirimatea blew soft his winds through the grasses of the hill, there the oldest tohunga paused and said, 'I feel your winds, Tawhirimatea. I feel your winds blow soft over the hill. I see your winds, Tawhirimatea. I see your winds toss the waves, toss and curl the waves of the bay so they swirl and fall green and white and blue in the bay.'

And deep beneath the waters of the bay, the oldest tohunga knew there dwelled Marakihau, Marakihau the awful taniwha of the sea, Marakihau, part fish, part man, all terrible Marakihau who comes up through the waves to suck down canoes and fisher-folk through his awful hollow tongue, sucks them down so they are seen no more in the world of men. 'Ae, Marakihau, terrible Marakihau, he and the waves of the sea, they also shall I pattern into the house so our people may know how terrible Marakihau may make the deep green sea.'

When the oldest tohunga was come to the great green forest of Tane, there in the cool places of the forest he saw the looped and folded fronds of fern, Pitau, the green springing unfolding fronds of fern rising from the forest floor, and the tohunga said, 'Pitau, little curling Pitau fern, for all you do for the people, for the sleeping beds you give us, for the fern root food you give for our women to roast for us in the cooking fires, ae, little Pitau fern, you too shall I surely pattern into the House of the People.'

And swinging light as air in the cool of the forest was the web of Punga-werewere, Punga-werewere the grey little spider waiting quiet in her web for Purehua the dust soft moth to come fluttering by. 'And you also,' said the oldest Tohunga, 'you also, little Punga-werewere with your web that curtains our whares, you also shall I remember and your web shall I pattern into the house.'

And there in the forest of Tane, deep in the forest of Tane, the tohunga came to the dark lonely swamp, and in the soft mud of the swamp he saw the four-toed mark of Pakura the swamp hen, Pakura the long-legged high-stepping white-tailed swamp hen. 'Arara!' the oldest tohunga said. 'The four-toed mark of Pakura, this shall I surely pattern into the house. And the raupo reed and the rushes that stand tall in the swamp, these shall I also use in the house, use to make the house dry and warm, to hold back the chill winds of Tawhirimatea, to shed the cold winter rains that fall.'

Deeper in the forest, the oldest tohunga saw Kaka, Kaka the grey-green parrot, climbing slowly up a swinging rata vine, climbing slowly leg after leg, beak after leg, leg after beak, leg after leg up the rata vine, and the oldest tohunga said, 'You, Kaka, you who give of your soft warm feathers that our women may weave soft warm cloaks, you with your strong curved beak, you too shall I pattern into the house, into Te Whare o Nga Tangata Whenua. Your strong beak, this shall I truly pattern into the house.'

But in the deepest of all part of the forest
the oldest tohunga watched for Manaia,
Manaia the fierce bird-head man,
Manaia with his bird beak lips, Manaia
with his bird bright eye, but Manaia did
not come that way on that day. But the
oldest tohunga said, 'Manaia I shall
remember, Manaia with his fearful bird
lips and his awful bird eye, Manaia too
shall I carve into the house Te Whare o
Nga Tangata Whenua.'

And as the oldest tohunga stayed quiet in the forest, the soft rains came, the soft tears of sorrow of the sky father Rangi, falling to wash on the earth mother Papa below. 'Aue!' the oldest tohunga said. 'The tears of Rangi, the love tears of Rangi for Papa below, these shall I also pattern into Te Whare o Nga Tangata Whenua.'

Now the time was come for the oldest tohunga to return to the kainga, and when he was back he called to him the other tohunga and he said, 'Tena koutou! I have searched over all Papa-tu-a-nuku, over all the body of the earth mother Papa, over all the earth stretching afar. In the forests, by the swamp, on the long sandy beach Taoneroa have I searched, and in my searching I have found many things that I shall tell for you to pattern into Te Whare o Nga Tangata Whenua, into the House of the People.' And he told them and he said, 'Now, you the tohunga of carving, and you of weaving, and you of pattern painting, it is for you to call your workmen, to call the old women and the maidens of the kainga, to carve for it, to weave for it, to pattern and paint for it, that this our house may be a fine house, a house that all the people of this our land Aotearoa will know.'

And the tohunga listened and they said, 'Eia! We have listened, and these things you have told us, these things we shall pattern into the house.'

'Now one thing more,' the oldest tohunga said, 'high above the house, in the front high place of the house, there shall be Tekoteko, Tekoteko standing tall and high on the house. And the people, when they see Tekoteko, will know how Tangaroa, god of the sea, stole our ancestor Te Manu-hauturuki from the land of men and placed him high on Tangaroa's house in the sea. So will I place Tekoteko high on the house so the people will know that the Tekoteko carving was of the first carving, of the carving learned from Tangaroa, god of the sea.'

Then the tohunga with their helpers went to their workplaces in the kainga and the days and weeks went by, so Marama the moon was grown many times to be Marama-the-great-mouthed-moon and lessened many times to Marama-the-moon-of-light-faintly-seen. And when the months had gone by so the winds of Tawhirimatea had chilled to winter and warmed again to spring, when the tears of Rangi had been soft summer showers and had hardened once more to raw winter rain, when the great spouting fish of Tangaroa, Pakeke the great whale out in the bay, had gone and come and gone again, when all these times had been, then the oldest tohunga called one day to the people of the kainga, saying, 'It is done! This our house, Te Whare o Nga Tangata Whenua, this the House of the People is done!'

Then the people of the kainga, when they saw the house, looked long at the house and in their looking they saw patterned into the house those things the oldest tohunga had seen in the forest of Tane. They saw the things he had seen on the long sandy beach Taoneroa, the things he had seen by the quiet lonely swamps.

In the warm red wood of totara they saw carved the terrible form of Marakihau with his long curved hollow tongue, and Manaia the bird-head man looked out fierce from the front of the house.

They saw carved the curl of Pitau the springing fern, with the web of Punga-werewere and the four-toe mark of Pakura and the long great shape of Pakeke the whale, Pakeke the great spouting fish of Tangaroa.

And the scale marks of Ika-moana, Ika-moana the children of Tangaroa, these the people saw also, the scale marks carved into totara from the forest of Tane.

And in the house the people saw the panels of tukutuku, tukutuku woven of raupo reeds and rushes from the edge of the still dark swamp. And woven in the tukutuku they saw the pattern of Patiki the flounder, with the soft rain-tears of Rangi and the terrible taniwha teeth of Marakihau.

And when the people looked high to the roof of the house, to the great rib rafters of the house, there on the rafters, painted in patterns of red of white and of black, were the painted patterns of kowhaiwhai. And in the kowhaiwhai were the beak of Kaka, the thin slice pattern of Marama the moon, the coil of Pitau, and the flat fish shape of Patiki the flounder.

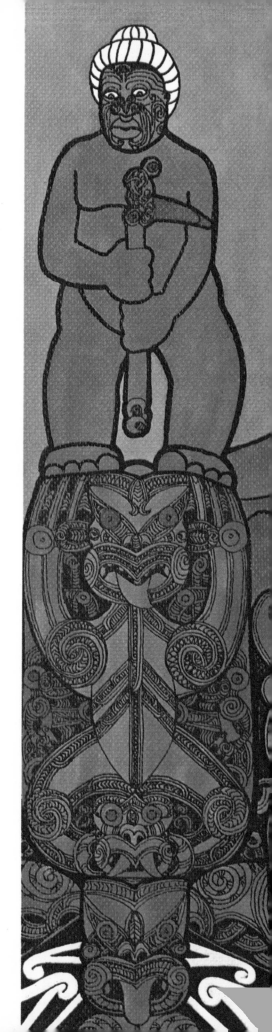

And high over all, in the front high place of the house, there was Tekoteko, Tekoteko standing tall on the house, watching the house and the people on the marae.

And the people of the kainga said, 'Eai! Now we have a marae and on this our marae we have a fine meeting house, and all the people through all the land will know that this is our house, our house Te Whare o Nga Tangata Whenua. This truly is the House of the People!'

Reycraft Books
55 Fifth Avenue
New York, NY 10003

Reycraftbooks.com

Reycraft Books is a trade imprint and trademark of Newmark Learning, LLC.

This edition is published by arrangement with China Children's Press & Publication Group Co., Ltd.
© China Children's Press & Publication Group Co., Ltd.
English translation provided by China Children's Press & Publication Group Co., Ltd.

Educators and Librarians: Our books may be purchased in bulk for promotional, educational,
or business use. Please contact sales@reycraftbooks.com.

This is a work of fiction. Names, characters, places, dialogue, and incidents described either are
the product of the author's imagination or are used fictitiously. Any resemblance to actual
persons, living or dead, is entirely coincidental.

Library of Congress Control Number: 2021914705

ISBN: 978-1-4788-7532-1

Printed in Dongguan, China. 8557/0721/18155

10 9 8 7 6 5 4 3 2 1

First Edition Hardcover published by Reycraft Books 2021.

Reycraft Books and Newmark Learning, LLC support diversity and the First Amendment,
and celebrate the right to read.

REYCRAFT
BOOKS